Syrenka

Stephen Oravec

Cablepunk Press

Oregon, Ohio

Syrenka

Syrenka lost her legs as a loyalist soldier in Typhon's Civil War. Before the shrapnel tore through her legs, however, she saved the life of the Prince, pulling his unconscious body from his downed helicopter out of the River Echidna and dragging it through heavy bombardment to the nearby Temple of Air. There she quickly sang a prayer to the Daughters of Air and left the Prince alone on the marble floor to return to the conflict, not realizing at the time she had fallen for him.

Her story went unbelieved, the hospital staff passing off her rescuing of the Prince as the ramblings of a shell-shocked double amputee. The clerics of the Temple of Air took credit for the Prince's beating heart, and they were richly rewarded by the Royal Family. Syrenka, however, poor before the War, poor and disabled after it, ended back in government housing, her neighbors likewise disabled and discarded veterans of the War. But though Typhon had abandoned her, Syrenka still loved Typhon, and she longed to be loved by the Prince.

Syrenka heard the key in the lock, and the door to her tiny, sparsely furnished apartment opened. Cumae stepped inside, soaked, carrying Syrenka's groceries. Syrenka had been staring at the wall, something she often did for hours on end, and climbed off the couch onto her skateboard. Her hands bare against the concrete, she paddled into the kitchen corner.

"Thank you, Cumae," Syrenka said. "I wouldn't have asked you to go out if I knew it was going to rain."

"Storm came out of nowhere," Cumae said. She set a bag on the floor. Syrenka unpacked the items into a cupboard beside the stove as Cumae put the groceries from another bag into the refrigerator.

"Did you get the protein drinks?" Syrenka asked.

"Yeah, they're in this bag here," Cumae said, setting a third bag from the counter down before Syrenka. "I got you a magazine as well. Lots of pictures of the Prince in there. Might've gotten a bit wet though."

"Thank you," said Syrenka, "but you shouldn't have. I don't have the money."

"My treat," said Cumae.

"But you don't have the money either," said Syrenka.

"Don't tell me what I do or do not have, dear," said Cumae.

Syrenka looked up to see what the expression was on Cumae's face, but she could not tell.

"There's apparently another Feast tonight down at the Water Palace," Cumae said. "Our district this time. The Prince is still searching for his bride-to-be. I don't know where they get the money."

Syrenka had flipped to the pictures of the Prince in the magazine.

"I have to get going," Cumae said. "I have to take my pills and rest."

"Do you still have plenty?" Syrenka asked.

"I'm starting to get low," Cumae said. "This weekend perhaps we can get some more?"

"Sounds good," Syrenka said.

Cumae crouched and handed Syrenka her keys. She brushed some of Syrenka's unkempt hair from her face. "You call me if you need anything, okay?" She smiled.

Syrenka smiled back. "Okay," she said. "Have a nice rest."

After Cumae had left, Syrenka reached up to lock the door. She, too, felt she needed a nap, and she couldn't imagine the pain Cumae must be experiencing. Syrenka hated to burden Cumae, but Cumae was the only person in the building who had even bothered to notice Syrenka. As all the tenants were in need, she had once foolishly believed they all would band together, veterans as they were of the War. Instead, it seemed to Syrenka, most of the tenants resented one another.

Syrenka climbed onto her couch and admired the pictures of the Prince in the magazine. Illiterate, she was clueless as to what the captions read. A few of the pictures were of a previous Feast and showed many well-dressed women dancing before the Prince, hoping to win his affection. Syrenka thought about what Cumae had said about the Feast being for their district this time. When Syrenka was a child, her mother realized she naturally excelled in song and dance and spent what little money they had sending Syrenka to the best song and dance schools in Typhon. Until drafted into the military four years ago at the age of fourteen, Syrenka had earned what meager money she could singing and dancing for tourists in the Market Square. That all seemed so long ago now. Putting down the magazine and resting her head, she thought about those days, confident the Prince would fall for her if only he heard her sing and saw her dance. She closed her eyes.

When Syrenka awoke, she had made up her mind. Having repeatedly helped Cumae acquire medicine she could not afford, she knew there were pills and potions out there that could do extraordinary and forbidden things. One such concoction she had thought about for more than a year, and she knew where she could get it.

The rain had stopped. Syrenka thought about calling Cumae on the telephone, but she knew Cumae would only try to stop her. Trusting Cumae, Syrenka had once before brought up the subject with her. Cumae had only scolded her for even thinking such a forbidden thought and hurriedly had changed the subject.

Syrenka steered around puddles on her way to the tram stop, her hands wet and dirty from the pavement. The July air was hot and humid, and she felt sticky as she waited on the tram. After ten minutes' time, the Blue Line tram arrived, and Syrenka boarded it, relieved it was one of the newer, low-floor trams about which many of her fellow citizens complained. No one was willing to give up their seat for her, and Syrenka knew many of them thought her either a pick-pocket or bum. She sat on the dirty and wet floor for fifteen stops before she managed to get a seat.

Looking out the windows, Syrenka watched as the city gave way to apple and pear orchards, and, then, at the end of the line, loomed the city's azoth liquefaction plant. Disembarking the tram, Syrenka headed down the road to the river, the smell of the plant making her nauseous. Ahead, at the port, a ship unloaded azoth into one of five great silos. Syrenka took a dilapidated road right and headed towards the Cemetery of the Nameless.

Syrenka knew Sibyl the river witch lived somewhere beyond the Cemetery, but she knew not where, and she grew nervous she would not be able to find her hut. Just past the Cemetery, the pothole-ridden road ended in a cul-de-sac, and all around the area was overgrown. Syrenka could see no path. Above, dark clouds had rolled back in. A cool breeze blew. She regretted not bringing her jacket.

Something wrapped itself around her torso, and she was pulled off her skateboard. Syrenka screamed, becoming aware it was a thick green vine which was dragging her into the overgrowth. She fumbled for her pocketknife with her right hand. Another vine wrapped around her right arm and pulled her in the opposite direction. Syrenka screamed again, trying for her knife with her left hand, as a third vine wrapped around her neck.

Then there was rot and decay, and the vines were gone. Syrenka looked up to see a pale, young woman in a black robe standing before her.

"Such a foolish girl," the woman said.

Syrenka didn't care for the comment as the woman could barely have been older than her. However, knowing the young woman had just saved her life, she kept her displeasure to herself.

"Thank you," Syrenka said instead. "Please," she said, getting back onto her skateboard, "do you know where the river witch lives?"

"Of course," said the young woman. "Follow me."

Syrenka followed the young woman down a well-trodden path towards the river, unsure at first how she had missed the path before. However, though she knew next to nothing of magic, she knew there was great magic at work all around, and she felt it growing stronger and stronger as they neared the river.

In a clearing at the river sat a wooden hut, a blackened apple tree with withered fruit beside it. Green smoke spiraled from the chimney. Syrenka expected the young woman to knock, but instead she opened the door. Syrenka went to call out, to prevent the young woman from entering, but stopped herself. "You're Sibyl," Syrenka said.

"Of course I am," said Sibyl, entering the hut. "Had I been anyone else, you'd already be dead, your bones sucked clean."

Sibyl turned and looked down to Syrenka who had followed her inside. Syrenka looked up.

"I—" Syrenka began.

"I know what you want," said the river witch, passing behind Syrenka and closing the door. "It is very stupid of you, but you are young."

Not liking the comment, Syrenka opened her mouth to retort, but then closed it, not wanting to irritate or anger the river witch. She had heard of Sibyl's numerous powers, many of which she had doubted. Now, in her company, Syrenka wasn't so sure the tales were false. Having grown a bit frightened, Syrenka eyed the knob on the door.

Sibyl caught her glance and smiled. The river witch headed to the fireplace where, despite it being summer, a large fire roared. She peered into a black cauldron then turned back to Syrenka. "Shall we?" she asked.

It was then Syrenka eyed the corpse of a young woman on the table.

"Poor girl washed ashore this morning," said Sibyl. "I must bury her in the Cemetery. Eventually. Pay her no mind."

Syrenka started to roll towards the door. The wheels on the wooden floor sounded abnormally loud to her.

"Shall we?" Sibyl asked again.

"Shall we what?" Syrenka asked.

Sibyl sighed. "You are here for legs to attend the Feast and dance for our Prince so that he may fall in love with you as you have fallen for him, and though you are very stupid to want this, I will help you, as it is my way," the river witch said. "Shall we begin?"

"What's your fee?" asked Syrenka.

"Only that I must take your tongue for the draught to work," said Sibyl.

"What?" asked Syrenka.

"My dear, you must understand that such magic is no trifling matter. If you wish to walk, you must become mute," Sibyl said. "A disability for a disability."

"But why my tongue?" Syrenka asked, sweating. "How will I convince the Prince to love me if I cannot speak!"

"My dear, the Prince is merely a man," Sibyl said. "Your beautiful body, your graceful dance, your . . . willingness. I'm sure you will find a way to ensnare his heart. What? Have you lost your courage?"

"No," said Syrenka, though she was not sure. She felt intoxicated. The room was warm. She looked to the fire.

"Good," said Sibyl. "But know one more thing. This magic will work for a month from the moment you first drink of the draught."

Syrenka nodded.

"Oh, but it is not what you think," said the river witch. "For if the Prince does not express his love for you in a month's time, you will become mine and transform into a fish, which I will gut and consume."

Syrenka felt revolted. "I think I'll be leaving," she said.

"What?" asked Sibyl. "Do you not believe in yourself? Do you think your fate is to end up a fish?"

Syrenka knew she had no other option in life to win the heart of the Prince, and it was this she wanted more than anything. "Very well," she said.

"Good," said Sibyl. "Climb up onto the table," she said, going into the kitchen to retrieve a glass. "Oh, do not be afraid of the corpse. She is quite dead at the moment. Take off your shorts, please."

Syrenka, atop the table, the corpse behind her, came to realize she had nothing appropriate with her to wear to the Feast. "I will need a dress. And shoes," she said as Sibyl scooped a thick green liquid out of the cauldron and poured it into the glass.

"My dear, I am not your fairy godmother," the river witch said. "You can take the dress and shoes of that poor dead girl behind you."

Syrenka turned to look over the corpse. "I'm not sure if they'll fit," she said, turning back as Sibyl handed her the glass.

"They fit," said Sibyl. "Drink."

Syrenka began to drink of the draught. "It's so cold!" she screamed.

"Yes, it's amazing how quickly it cools," Sibyl said. "Drink. You have less than a month's time."

Syrenka downed the thick, green liquid. She set the glass on the table. She was shivering, but at the sight of the knife in Sibyl's right hand she forgot how cold she was.

"Stick out your tongue," said Sibyl.

Syrenka looked into the river witch's deep green eyes. She stuck out her tongue.

Quickly, Sibyl grabbed the tip of Syrenka's tongue and cut it out. Syrenka, now dumb, screamed. Blood gushed from her mouth. The river witch dropped the severed tongue into the glass and drove the blood-covered knife into Syrenka's right leg. Blood flowed from the wound as Sibyl withdrew the knife. Syrenka tried to get away from Sibyl across the table.

"Hold still!" shouted the river witch, "or you'll be hopping!" Syrenka stopped, and Sibyl drove the knife into her left leg.

Blood spilling from three painful wounds, Syrenka fell on her side on the table and cried. She watched Sibyl lick the blood off the knife and set it down beside the glass. Then Sibyl picked up Syrenka's skateboard.

"This object of your disability you will need no more," Sibyl said, carrying it to the fire. She tossed the skateboard into the flames.

Syrenka screamed as her stumps burst open, green liquid bubbling from the ruptures. At first,

Syrenka thought something had gone wrong, but then two long, shapely legs formed in the blink of an eye. The pain was gone. Wearily she sat up, admiring her new pair of legs.

"Such a mess," Sibyl said. She waved her open palm before the fireplace. White, cold foam overflowed the cauldron and scoured the floor and table. Syrenka felt goose bumps break out on her newly formed legs as the foam licked the table clean of her blood and withdrew. "Well?" the river witch asked.

Syrenka slid off the table and stood on her new legs. She stepped forward, expecting to experience some difficulty, but she did not. She walked, twirled, and smiled at the river witch.

"Good," said Sibyl. "Now take the dress and shoes from that poor dead girl and be gone with you. Charon awaits you at the river and will take you to the Feast."

Syrenka nodded, rushing to the corpse and undressing her.

"Dance and be merry," said the river witch, placing the glass with Syrenka's tongue in an ice chest.

Syrenka found the corpse's red dress to be the perfect length, and the black flats fit perfectly as well. She looked upon the naked body of the dead girl whose skin was as white as snow. Syrenka wondered for a moment who she was, feeling guilty she had robbed the corpse of its clothes. Then she felt Sibyl's left hand on her left shoulder. With her right hand, the river witch zipped up the dress Syrenka now wore.

"Fail to win the Prince's love and I will come for you," Sibyl said, turning Syrenka around to face her. "Now go. Charon awaits."

Syrenka nodded and left the hut. At the river she found the boatman Charon standing on the bank, a rustic rowboat motionless in the water behind it. Without a word, the burly figure picked up Syrenka as she approached. She stared into the creature's flickering blue eyes of flame as it carried her through the shallow water to the wooden boat, gently placing her in it. Charon ascended and sat at the back. Without word or oar, the boat headed out to deeper water. In silence, the two traveled upstream.

The sun was setting as they passed the port, and some motorboats passed them heading up the river as well, but Syrenka noticed they went unnoticed, and their small wooden boat passed through the wake of each motorboat as if they were gliding through calm water. Syrenka felt uncomfortable in the silence, and though she dared to speak, she could not. Curious, she opened her mouth and stuck her fingers in, but she hastily withdrew them at the absence of her tongue. She thought she would retch. Remembering Sibyl with the knife, she focused her thoughts instead on the Prince. She smiled. Tonight she would dance for him. Tonight he would fall in love with her. The breeze was warm. She was happy.

Soon they reached the point where the Echidna Canal flowed into the Echidna. A police boat sat at anchor, yet they slipped into the Canal unnoticed. Syrenka looked to an officer on the boat ten feet from her. Oblivious, he gazed at the Echidna beyond. As they headed further up the Canal where police boats patrolled, the sky growing dark, the trees thick on either side, Syrenka grew nervous and turned to Charon.

"I am Charon," the boatman said, responding to the expression on Syrenka's face. "I go where I please."

Syrenka nodded and turned forward. Lights from the River Palace soon lit up the Canal ahead. Once, as a girl, Syrenka had visited the River Palace with her mother on some holiday. Down through

Lamia Park they had to walk and then across a small bridge to the island on which the Palace was built. Syrenka could see people crossing that bridge now as the boat headed to the bank of the Canal. Between two thick trees a stone stairway rose out of the water. Charon guided the boat alongside it.

The boatman stood. The boat did not rock. Syrenka stood and stepped out onto the wet stairway. She turned to thank Charon with a smile, but the boatman had departed.

With no way to thank Charon, Syrenka ascended the steep steps and passed through the undergrowth to a stone path. It was dark under the canopy and few lampposts illuminated the way. She headed towards the bridge.

"Where did you come from?" a guard exclaimed as she neared.

"No doubt crawled out of the sewers like the rest of this lot," another guard said. "The riffraff we've gotten tonight! Why the Prince would even bother?"

Angry at the comment, Syrenka pointed to the military barcode on her neck.

"Yeah, I've got one too," the guard said. "Get moving across the bridge."

At first fuming at the injustice, Syrenka's cheer returned as she crossed the bridge and heard music. The doors to the windowed hall where the Feast was being held were open, light and jubilance streaming into the summer night. Upon entering, Syrenka saw women of all classes and attire feasting at the tables while in the center of the room numerous others danced, some together, some alone. The Prince sat at the head table, mostly uninterested in the dancers as Syrenka watched him, eating and in conversation with the men around him. She noticed that while many of the neglected dancers were enjoying the company of one another, others grew frustrated and gave up their dance, some returning to the tables, some leaving the hall.

"Such a pig of a man," one such woman said as she passed Syrenka.

Syrenka walked to the center of the hall and began to dance. She glided and twirled and dared once to leap, becoming aware that many in the hall began to turn their gaze towards her. Soon, the Prince watched as she performed, and the floor cleared, and she alone danced, enchanting the Prince. He came down from the dais to her, applauding her, and the whispers began that the Prince had found his bride.

But it wasn't so. The Prince made Syrenka a page, and for nearly a month the two were inseparable. They spent their days swimming in the waters of the River Palace, riding horseback through the Royal Forest, and strolling quietly through the Royal Palace Gardens. Syrenka danced daily for him, sometimes clothed, many times not, and they spent their nights coupled in bed, Syrenka feeling more than once she was compromising herself for the many desires of the Prince. But during the days she loved him and considered herself the happiest she had ever been. Not once, however, did the Prince tell Syrenka he loved her, and, as the month wore on and Syrenka became unable to sexually please the Prince to his liking, she began to sense the Prince was losing interest in her.

The morning arrived of the final day of the month's time and still the Prince had not told Syrenka he loved her. For the past three days she hadn't even seen him. At the entrance to the Royal Palace Gardens, she sat on a bench waiting for him, tossing a golden ball up high and catching it, hoping he had not forgotten her. He did arrive, late, and Syrenka could tell something was amiss. She stood and smiled at the Prince.

"My dumb foundling," the Prince said, kissing her on the cheek. "Thank you for waiting. Shall we?"

The two entered the Gardens, and it was some time before the Prince spoke. "Your devotion to me has been great," he began, "so you will rejoice at my news: I've found my bride!"

Syrenka felt her heart sink.

"Or, rather, she found me," the Prince said.

Syrenka felt she would cry, but no tears came. Her legs grew heavy as they walked.

"My father thought I would find my bride at the Feasts as he had done," the Prince began, "but he did not know I had already fallen for another. The clerics of the Temple of Air claim to have saved my life, and so my father would have the city believe. But I've always known it was none of the clerics of Typhon. Her face I vaguely remember, but I remember all too well her voice. She sang to the Daughters of Air for me. When you danced at the Feast, I thought, what luck, you could be her. But how could you be, my dumb foundling? I began to wonder if she was even real, if I had imagined it all, after all. Or perhaps she was an angel? But she is real, and I've heard her sing! She had been a visiting cleric from Ophion stranded here during the Eastern Siege. I know my father will oppose the wedding, and so I've arranged for us to be secretly married at the Temple of Air tonight. I know you are overjoyed for me. Know that you will always have a place here at the Palace."

They had walked in a circle just inside the Gardens, and now they stopped before the exit. Syrenka wanted to get away.

"I must be off," the Prince said. "There is still much to do. Be at the Temple of Air at sundown for the ceremony." He turned and left.

Syrenka ran crying through the Gardens, getting lost in the hedge maze. Eventually, in a clearing, she threw herself down on a bench beside a little pond in the shadow of a statue of the Prince, sobbing. She thought she would hide in the maze, away from everyone, away from the river witch. She thought back to a month ago, how the river witch had given her legs, how she had hoped to win the love of the Prince, how the sacrifice of her tongue, of her song, had all been for nothing.

Then she remembered Cumae.

Syrenka's head swirled. She stood and lost her balance, falling onto the grass. The golden ball plunked into the pond. Syrenka stood again and ran, her alarm only increasing as she came to one dead end after another in the maze. The sun was low and her frustration and concern high when she finally made it out of the maze. She ran into the Palace and picked up the nearest wall-mounted telephone, frantically keying Cumae's number, getting it wrong each time. Eventually, she correctly recalled the sequence of buttons, but the phone did not ring, the number disconnected, the bill gone unpaid.

"Is there something the matter?" Heinrich, Captain of the Palace Guard, asked as he approached. "You look distraught."

Syrenka turned from him. She ran from the Palace and to the gate, hurrying to the nearby tram stop. She wasn't even sure the line to take, and she could not read the map.

An aged hag accosted her. "You want the Red Line, dear," she said. Syrenka pulled away from the hag's grip, but when she looked into her face, she saw it was instead the young face of the river witch Sibyl. "You want the Red Line, dear," the river witch repeated, "but it will do no good."

The Red Line tram arrived. Syrenka boarded. Sibyl remained on the platform.

The tram traveled slowly, and Syrenka cursed herself and all of Typhon in silence on the slow journey. The sun was behind the buildings as she arrived at her apartment building, and she knew the hour of her doom was near. There was an ambulance before the building. Syrenka began to run.

The door to Cumae's apartment was open. The paramedics wheeled out a body on a stretcher under a sheet. They wore masks. Syrenka thought the smell would make her sick. She turned and quickly exited the building.

Near the entrance, Sibyl stood in the grass under a willow tree. Syrenka thought about running, but she knew there was no place she could hide from the river witch and her magic. She approached the river witch.

"I told you it would do no good," Sibyl said.

Syrenka opened her mouth to curse Sibyl. She made a fist.

From beneath her robe, Sibyl pulled out a knife, the same knife she had used to sever Syrenka's tongue. Syrenka stopped.

"I've decided to offer you a way out," Sibyl said. "But you have very little time left. Here, take this knife. Three stops down the Yellow Line will bring you to the Temple of Air. Kill the Prince and you will be free from me, your transformation canceled, your death delayed."

Syrenka took the knife. She thought about slaying Sibyl with it but knew the river witch to be too powerful.

"Hate me all you want, dear," said Sibyl, "but I have offered you a way out. You don't have much time."

Syrenka slipped away the knife and turned for the tram stop.

Shortly she disembarked onto the platform near the Temple of Air, and she rushed through moving traffic to the building's grounds. She glanced down to the spot in the River Echidna from which she had pulled the Prince.

A cleric approached Syrenka as she entered the Temple. "Ah, you are the Prince's page," the cleric said. "They're at the top of the central tower. The elevator is just over there."

Syrenka bowed her head and walked across the marble floor to the tower's elevator. Her legs began to pain her as she waited on the elevator, and she leaned against the wall. Stepping into the elevator, she collapsed as the door slid shut behind her. Syrenka reached and pressed the button to ascend to the tower's top, forcing herself to stand as the door opened. Walking tormented her, and she did her best to hide the pain from her face as she passed two guards standing on either side of the doorway to the tower's balcony. As she entered the balcony, she passed a priest exiting it. The marriage ceremony was over. Syrenka stumbled. The wind wailed.

At the railing, their backs turned to Syrenka, stood the Prince and his bride. Syrenka drew the river witch's knife and quickened her pace, closing the distance as the pain in her legs shocked her, twisting her torso. Her trousers felt damp and clung. Over the wind, she heard the Prince's bride talking. She vaguely recognized the voice as her own.

The Prince turned.

Syrenka slashed. Aiming for the Prince's neck, she stumbled, slicing him instead across the face. Screaming and blinded, the Prince fell to the floor, clutching the cut.

"Guards!" the Prince cried.

Syrenka looked to the Prince's bride, and she recognized at once the face wrapped in white cleric garb.

"Kill him, my little fish," mouthed the river witch Sibyl.

The doors to the balcony swung opened. "Freeze!" yelled the guards in unison.

Syrenka dropped the knife, climbed onto the railing, and jumped. The wind caught her. Gently it carried her down to the Echidna. At the spilling of the Prince's blood, Sibyl's magic had been warped, and into the river Syrenka slipped, her upper body human, her lower the tail of a fish.

www.ingramcontent.com/pod-product-compliance
Lightning Source LLC
Chambersburg PA
CBHW050920120626
46552CB00004B/1682